Pat Hutchins

RED FOX

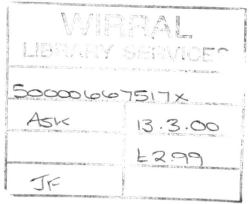
A Red Fox Book

Published by Random House Children's Books
20 Vauxhall Bridge Road, London SW1V 2SA

A division of Random House UK Ltd
London Melbourne Sydney Auckland
Johannesburg and agencies throughout the world

Copyright © Pat Hutchins 1999
Copyright © photographs Hutchins Film Company Limited

A Hutchins Film Company Limited production for Yorkshire Television

1 3 5 7 9 10 8 6 4 2

First published by Red Fox 1999

Printed and bound in Hong Kong.

RANDOM HOUSE UK Limited Reg. No. 954009

ISBN 0 09 940232 7

Titch was very pleased. His best friend, Sam, was coming round.
   They were going to play with the balloon.

Just then, the phone rang.
It was Sam's mum saying
Sam couldn't come over
after all.

And then the balloon burst.
    So Titch didn't even have a balloon to play with.

'Will you play with me?' Titch asked Peter and Mary. 'We can't,' they said. 'We're going to the football match with Dad.'

So Titch had no one to play with.

'I know,' said Mum. 'Let's go for a picnic in the park. You can go and fetch the old blanket to sit on, and the ball to play with.'

Titch went upstairs to find the blanket and the ball.

The blanket was on top of the cupboard.

But when Titch pulled the blanket down, the ball went bouncing away!

So he went into his bedroom
to look for it.

He didn't find the ball, but he found his old railway set that he hadn't played with for a long time.

'I'd like to play with that again,' thought Titch. 'I'll take it on the picnic.'

He still couldn't find the ball, but he found lots of old toys he'd like to take on the picnic.

Titch piled all the toys onto the blanket and took them downstairs.

'Titch!' said Mum. 'We can't carry all those toys to the park, you'll have to leave them at home.'

Titch put his coat on. Tailcat didn't want him to go out.

'I'll be back soon, Tailcat,' said Titch.

But then there was a big crash of thunder that frightened Tailcat. And then came the sound of rain.

'Dear me!' said Mum. 'Just listen to that rain!
It's pouring down. We won't be able to have our
picnic after all!'

But then Mum had an idea.

  'Yes we can!' she said. 'We can have our picnic in the front room!'

  Titch thought this was a good idea.

So Mum put the sandwiches and
the lemonade on the blanket,
and they had a lovely picnic.

Then Titch set up his railway, and found the ball, which had bounced downstairs.

'We don't need the ball to play with now, do we, Tailcat?' said Titch. 'We've got all these other toys.'

And Titch and Tailcat really enjoyed
their indoor picnic.

9 Days of Piper Snow

written by
Daniella Blechner

illustrated by
Victor Onyenobi

Conscious Dreams
P U B L I S H I N G

9 Days of Piper Snow

First Printed in United Kingdom 2023

Published by Conscious Dreams Publishing
www.consciousdreamspublishing.com

Illustrated by Victor Onyenobi

Edited by Daniella Blechner

Typeset by Bryony Dick

ISBN: 978-1-915522-48-1

Dedication

For my readers, may you find joy, laughter and comfort between these pages.

This is for you, Dad. x

Samara glanced out of her window, looking really sad.
It was a year ago today that she lost her beloved dad.
She wished she could magic herself away to a faraway land,
where all she did was laugh and build castles in the sand.

'Come down to dinner. It's time to eat your food!'
Her mum called her down, but she wasn't in the mood.
She flicked her peas around her plate and picked at her dish.
She glanced across the table. There was one person that she missed.

When dinner was over, she trudged up the stairs full of gloom,

But nothing would prepare her for the guest inside her room.

She looked it in the eye, and it stood very still.

There it was as white as snow upon her windowsill.

He stared at her; she stared at him; he wasn't backing down.

His blue eyes transfixed on her eyes of deepest brown.

'Hello,' she said, curious. 'What are you doing here?'

He cooed at her as if a long-lost friend or someone very dear.

'Mum! Come quickly! Look at this!' she cried.

In a flash, her mum was standing by her side.

'What is it, Samara? There's nothing there,' Mum said.

'There was a white pigeon right here with grey feathers on its head!'

The next day, Samara couldn't stop thinking
about the visitor in her room.
She couldn't concentrate at school. Will the bell ring soon?
When school was over, she rushed home excited.
If the white pigeon was there, she wouldn't be happy,
she'd be delighted!

She burst into her room and there he was
peeping through her windowpane.
She whispered softly through the glass,
'Hello there. What's your name?'
He cooed at her and puffed out his neck; something male pigeons do.
She smiled at him, her first smile in months
and her love for him then grew.

She opened the window just a crack and softly said,
'I've had a really sad day.'
The pigeon watched quietly, cocked his head
and tapped his beak where her head lay.
She held her hand out through the crack, trying to make friends.
But he pecked her finger, which hurt a bit
— it's just the way that he defends.

The next day, she bought some sunflower seeds on her way home from school.
She thought if he was hungry, feeding him would be cool.
And there he was upon her ledge, waiting for a feed.
She fed him on her windowsill the entire packet of seeds!

He pecked and pecked. He would not stop. He was a greedy fellow.
'Don't feed the bird!' the neighbour shouted in a rather loud bellow.
'He's my friend!' Samara said. 'He listens when I talk.'
The pigeon stood there proudly and added in a squawk.

'He'll never leave if you feed him, Samara.
He's vermin and disease-ridden!'
'Does your mum know about this bird,
or is it a secret that you've hidden?'

Her mum burst in!
'What on earth is that? Get it off the sill!'
The pigeon stood, chest beating fast,
but standing very still.

'Please, Mum! He's really sweet.
He won't do any harm!' she cried.
Mum looked at her daughter.
It had been a long time
since she'd seen her smile so wide.
'Ok Samara, but get it outside now!'
The pigeon bopped its head and gave a little bow.

For six more days, the pigeon came, and she named him Piper Snow.
Everywhere Samara went, the pigeon would surely go.
He followed her to school,
whispered maths answers outside the class.
She started to enjoy school again, and her sadness slowly passed.

Then one day Piper didn't come to visit her at her window!
Samara looked and looked, but he didn't come. Where did Piper go?
She waited again until bedtime and then again tomorrow.
Samara felt her tears well up and she was filled with so much sorrow.

And then one day as she went to school,
she saw the old neighbours fixing the windscreen wiper.
She stopped to say hello and there was her bird, Piper!
'This is our bird 'Porri',' said Mr Miah. 'We missed him oh so much,'
'We moved out two weeks ago, and we have since lost touch.'

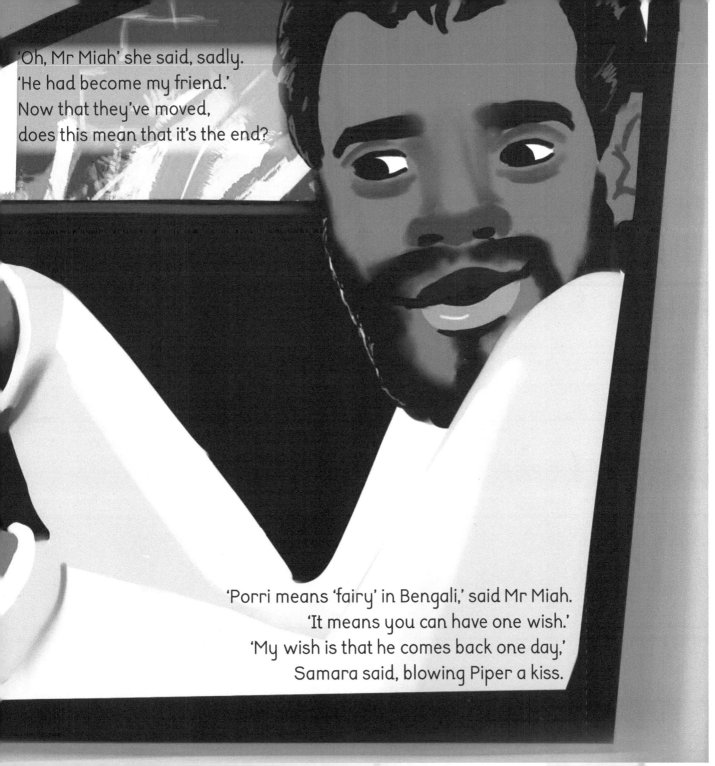

'Oh, Mr Miah' she said, sadly.
'He had become my friend.'
Now that they've moved,
does this mean that it's the end?

'Porri means 'fairy' in Bengali,' said Mr Miah.
'It means you can have one wish.'
'My wish is that he comes back one day,'
Samara said, blowing Piper a kiss.

That evening she sat by her window remembering 9 days of good times.

At least he is well looked after, he even fine dines.

Sometimes great things don't last forever, but the memory lives on

And if the memory is still alive, is anything ever really gone?

A few weeks later, Samara was in her bedroom
doing work for her English class.
When suddenly she heard a familiar tapping on her glass.
And there he was standing there, eyes shining and bold as brass.
'Piper!' she cried. 'I knew you'd be back!'
She laughed and laughed and laughed.

He cooed three times and bowed his head.
She stroked him and then softly said,
'You're free to go. Come back and visit me any day or any weather.'
He blinked and bowed and flew off again and left behind a feather.

In Loving Memory of my Dad
Ron Paul Blechner

About Piper

Piper is a real-life pigeon who mysteriously turned up on Daniella's office windowsill one bright sunny day in May 2023. He arrived just after she placed a photo of her dad on her windowsill. Having shocked both Daniella and her partner, Neville, he decided he was going to stay.

Since then, he tries to sneak in through the window on a daily basis and make himself at home.

Piper is a very determined pigeon with lots of personality and humour. He can also be very noisy. He likes to get up early and let everyone know that he is there, and he loves hemp seeds!

Piper enjoys playing the piano, helping Daniella write books and dancing on her head. He hopes to write his own book one day.

About the Author

Daniella is an author of nine books. She is a Book Journey Mentor and founder of Conscious Dreams Publishing. She has helped more than 200 people write and publish their own books, including authors as young as seven years old!

As a child, Daniella loved reading and telling stories to her sisters and anyone who would listen. She loves animals and nature and believes that if we listen closely enough to them, we can learn a lot.

Daniella is also an English teacher and loves inspiring young people to discover their own gifts and talents and describes working with them as 'magical'.

Daniella lives in Croydon with her partner, Neville, who is also her best friend and biggest supporter. They both, although they wouldn't admit it, live with a pigeon!

Acknowledgements

Thank you to my number one supporter and favourite person on the planet,
Nevile Butler, for putting up with me and my endless pigeon whispering.

Thank you to Piper for inspiring me!

Thank you to the Miah family for allowing me to have joint custody of the pigeon.

Thank you to Victor Onyenobi, the talented illustrator
who worked tirelessly to bring my vision to life.

Thank you to Bryony Dick who typeset this book
and weaved it all together seamlessly.

Thank you to Ces Price who designed the beautiful frames for my dad, Piper and I.

Lastly, thank you to you, yes YOU for reading and enjoying this book.

Conscious Dreams

PUBLISHING

Transforming diverse writers
into successful published authors

www.consciousdreamspublishing.com

authors@consciousdreamspublishing.com

Let's connect

Milton Keynes UK
Ingram Content Group UK Ltd.
UKHW050421171123
432729UK00002B/7